DOUG's™
Big
Comeback

BRAND SPANKING NEW!

Created by Jim Jinkins

Adapted by
Nancy E. Krulik

Illustrated by
Pete List and Cheng-li Chan, Tony
Curanaj, Chris Dechert, Brian Donnelly,
Ray Feldman, Chris Palesty, Matt
Peters, and Jonathan Royce

JUMBO
PICTURES
INC.

GRADE A QUALITY

DISNEY
PRESS

New York

Original Script by Dennis Garvey

Original Characters for "The Funnies"
Developed by Jim Jinkins and Joe Aaron

Printed in the United States of America.

First Edition

1 3 5 7 9 10 8 6 4 2

The text for this book is set in 16-point Berkeley Book.

Library of Congress Catalog Card Number: 96-71632

ISBN:0-7868-4150-8

Big
Comeback

Chapter 1

Crash!

"*Yes!*" Doug Funnie pumped his fist high in the air. All right! Another strike!

Doug's best friend, Skeeter Valentine, marked a big black *X* on the scorecard.

"Wow, Doug," Skeeter said. "You're burning 'em up today! This is the best game you ever bowled."

Now it was Skeeter's turn. He raced up to the line and sent his ball soaring down the lane. The ball rolled, and rolled, and . . . knocked down one pin. Skeeter turned to Doug and frowned.

But Doug smiled, "Way to go, Skeet. Knock down the rest of 'em and you get a spare!"

Skeeter stared down at the nine standing pins and gritted his teeth. He picked up his ball and rolled it down the alley. Six more pins dropped. Unfortunately, they dropped in someone else's lane.

Skeeter shrugged and slumped back to the scoring table. He studied the scorecard.

"Wow, Doug, if you get a strike, you beat your top score," Skeeter told him.

Doug knew that. He was imagining that he was a pro bowler, winning a big tournament and then being honored in a ticker-tape parade.

Of course, that was all inside his head, but Doug still wanted to beat his all-time high. Success was within his reach . . . until Roger Klotz and his pals showed up at the bowling alley.

As Doug got up to bowl, he saw Roger coming his way. "Oh great," Doug moaned. "Roger's really been riding me lately."

Sure enough, Roger stopped just behind Doug's lane. "Hey, guys, look," Roger shouted. "It's the gutter-ball boys."

"Don't pay any attention to him," Skeeter said. "He only does it because he thinks he's funny."

Doug nodded. He was *trying* to ignore Roger. But ignoring Roger was not the easiest thing to do. Doug stood at the line, held up his ball, and aimed. He was determined to show Roger what a good bowler he was.

"Hey, Funnie," Roger called out in a voice loud enough for everybody to hear. "Is that your head, or are you bowling with two balls?"

Doug was angry. He turned to Roger and

shouted in his toughest voice, *"Oh yeah?"*

Roger laughed. So did his friends. Doug couldn't blame them. "Oh yeah" *was* kind of a lame comeback.

Doug reached back and bowled. The ball clunked loudly into the gutter, bounced up, and flew across the bowling alley!

All over the building, bowlers yelled "Heads up!" or "Flying ball!"

Doug blushed. How *embarrassing*. Roger had done it to him again.

Chapter 2

That night at dinner, Doug told his family what had happened.

"I think the ball must've jumped about twelve lanes and it would've kept going if it hadn't lodged in Mr. Swirly's—"

Doug's older sister, Judy, burst out laughing. She laughed so hard her beret flipped right off her head. "Slapstick," she guffawed. "I love it! Dougie, our silent little clown."

Doug stared at Judy. For someone who claimed to be a sensitive artist, his sister could be really *in*sensitive. "It's not funny, Judy," Doug told her. "Roger's always raggin' on everybody. I wish I could shut him up once and for all!"

Doug's father shook his head. "I don't think you want to sink to Roger's level, son," he said. "Just ignore him and he'll get tired of teasing you."

"But don't worry, I never will," Judy snickered.

Doug's mother shot Judy a stern look. "Your brother has a problem, Judy. You shouldn't make fun." Then she turned to Doug. "I know what I would say to that Roger Klotz."

Doug was desperate. He'd take advice even from a grown-up! "What, Mom?" he asked.

Doug's mother looked him straight in the eye and said, "I'm rubber, you're glue. What you say bounces off of me and sticks to you. So there."

Doug actually considered it. The next day, as Doug and Skeeter walked to Swirly's for a shake, Doug told his buddy what his mother had advised. Skeeter wasn't so sure about the comeback. "You think that'll work, man?" he asked doubtfully.

"Well, it *is* kind of old," Doug agreed.

"Instead of glue, you could say that he's an electromagnet. That's pretty modern," Skeeter suggested.

Luckily, Doug didn't have to try the "I'm rubber, you're glue" line. Roger wasn't there. Doug and Skeeter sat down in a booth next to Chalky Studebaker.

They watched as Chalky moved french fries and ketchup packs all around the table. Chalky was so involved with rearranging the food, he didn't even realize Doug and Skeeter were sitting with him.

"Hey, Chalky," Doug said, finally.

"Oh hey, guys," Chalky mumbled as he moved two french fries over toward the salt shaker. "I'm working out plays for the big game against Bloatsburg. You guys coming?" Chalky was the player-coach for the Beebe

Bluff Middle School baseball team. Doug nodded. "I'll be there."

Skeeter frowned. "I'm on the team, Chalky; I've just never gotten to play. No wonder you forgot."

Chalky put down the salt shaker and looked seriously at Skeeter. "Sorry, Skeeter, I gotta go with the best players if we want to be the league champions."

"But Chalky, we're undefeated," Skeeter insisted. "We've won every game."

Chalky sighed. "But they weren't all shutouts," he explained. "There's still plenty of room for improvement." He went back to his game plans.

Skeeter gave up and went to the counter. "Doug, you want anything?" he called back. "I'm getting some fries."

Before Doug could answer, Roger, Willy, Boomer, and Ned stormed into Swirly's.

Roger spotted his first victim. "Don't eat too much, Valentine," he teased Skeeter. "You don't want to break the bench." Skeeter sighed and slumped up to the counter.

Roger and his friends sat down next to Doug and Chalky. And Patti Mayonnaise walked over, carrying a burger and fries. "Hey, Chalky; hey, Doug," she said.

Doug smiled. Patti was the girl of his dreams. He was crazy about her. He just didn't know how to tell her.

"Hey, Studebaker," Roger shouted. "You oughta put Funnie on your team. He'd really be great . . . at being a loser!"

Roger and his gang burst out laughing. Doug blushed beet red. Roger had burned him with an insult again. And this time it

9

was in front of Patti. Doug wasn't going to take it any more.

"You know something, Roger?" he said. "I'm an electromagnet and you're glue." Doug stopped for a minute and shook his head. That wasn't how it went. "No," he began again, "I'm iron and—"

Roger snickered. "Man, Funnie, your comebacks are as lame as your bowling."

Everyone looked at Doug. They were waiting for Doug to say something that would really put Roger in his place.

Doug glared at Roger. He wiped the sweat from his brow. He opened his mouth and blurted out, *"Oh yeah?"*

Chapter 3

Poor Doug. Roger was really driving him nuts. No place was safe. Not even school!

On Monday morning, Doug was sitting in Ms. Kristal's English class. Doug liked Ms. Kristal, so he wasn't that nervous—even though it was his day to give a book report.

When Ms. Kristal called his name, Doug stood and walked to the front of the room. But before he could speak, Roger started goofing on him.

"Duck and cover, everybody," Roger snarled. "Here comes a real bomb!"

"Roger, please," Ms. Kristal asked softly.

Doug gripped his paper tightly. If he wasn't nervous before, he sure was now. "The book I read was—"

"Probably one of those pop-up books for babies," Roger interrupted.

Doug gulped. "It was not," he defended himself. "It was a pretty cool book called—"

"Talk lower, Funnie," Roger interrupted again. "We can still hear you in the back."

Doug took a step backward. He wanted to get as far from Roger as he could. But as he leaned against the black-board, it collapsed. Doug jumped out of the way—and land-ed with his foot in the wastebasket. The whole class cracked up. Roger laughed the loudest.

If there was ever a time to get Roger, this was it. Doug stared at him. This called for a real comeback, but Doug could only think of one thing to say.

"Oh yeah?"

That after-
noon, Doug
went to Beebe
Field to watch
the big game.
He tried to
avoid Roger
as best he
could. But wherever Doug went, Roger
seemed to be, too. Roger and his gang even sat
two rows below him in the bleachers.

Still, even Roger couldn't stop Doug from
being happy at the game. Patti was on a roll.
She'd hit some long, hard drives, and even
made a diving catch that won the game for
the team. Doug was really proud of Patti.
When the game ended, he raced onto the
field to congratulate her.

The team was still undefeated. Doug figured Chalky had to be happy about that.

Doug figured wrong.

"What's the big deal?" Chalky asked Doug as he watched the other players cheer for Patti. "She almost missed the catch."

The team started walking away. But Chalky wasn't finished with them yet. "I'm calling practice in ten minutes. We've got to get ready for the interleague semifinals," he called to the players.

Patti turned and put her hands on her hips. "We won the game, Chalky. We're not practicing now. We're going to Swirly's."

"Okay, you're right," Chalky agreed. Patti smiled. She'd won that battle.

Almost.

"Be back in half an hour," Chalky told the team.

Patti shook her head. "See you *tomorrow*, Chalky," she shouted back, as she stormed off the field.

Roger, Willy, Ned, and Boomer made a tight circle around Doug. Doug started to sweat.

"Quite a big mouth on little Ms. Mayonnaise, huh Funnie?" Roger barked.

Patti walked by the crowd of boys. "Hey, Annie Oakley," Roger baited her, "way to shoot your mouth off!"

Patti ignored Roger. But Roger wasn't through with her yet. "What a loudmouth," he said to Doug. "I'd sure never let a girl talk to me that way."

Now Doug was mad. It was one thing for Roger to pick on him. But nobody— *nobody*—picked on Patti!

"I've never even seen a girl talk to you at all, Roger," Doug snapped.

Roger was shocked. His eyes opened

15

wide. He didn't say a word. Doug got nervous. And then, suddenly, Willy, Ned, and Boomer burst out laughing.

"Good one, Doug!" Boomer said. He patted Doug on the back.

"Yeah, nice burn, Funnie," Ned added.

Roger glared at his friends. He turned and stormed off in a huff. As he left, Doug could hear him mumbling:

"Oh yeah?"

Chapter 4

Doug was really proud of himself. He'd gotten Roger really bad! And making the other kids laugh felt pretty amazing. Best of all, he'd come to Patti's rescue. He was sort of like a superhero. *Funnieman!*

After dinner, Doug went up to his room. He was supposed to be doing his homework. But instead he was imagining what it would be like to be Funnieman. He could almost hear the announcer at the comedy club:

"Look! Up on the stage!" the announcer would say. "It's a juggler! It's a performance artist! It's . . . *Funnieman!* Yes, Funnieman, fighting a never-ending battle to defend the insulted."

As Funnieman, Doug could give his pals the comebacks they'd need to fight off the evil Roger.

If Roger told Patti that she was proof there was no intelligent life on the planet, Funnieman could come to her rescue and say, "Stand back, ma'am. No use trying to make him act like a human being. He doesn't do impressions." That would really sting Roger.

Doug smiled as he thought about it. He was the king of the comeback now! Doug was on a roll!

The next day, Roger really gave it to Skeeter.

"Nice outfit, Valentine," he said. "I used to dress like that . . . until my dad got a job!"

Doug smiled. It was time for Funnieman to swing into action. "Oh really? Your dad got a job?" Doug said sarcastically. "I didn't know the circus was in town!"

Everybody laughed. Then they waited for Roger to say something clever.

"Watch this," Willy whispered to Boomer. "Roger's gonna cream him!"

But much to everyone's surprise, Roger didn't cream Doug. All he said was, "*Oh yeah?* Well I don't have time to listen to your weak little jokes." Roger turned to Boomer, Ned, and Willy, "Come on, you guys."

But Boomer, Ned, and Willy didn't move

to follow Roger. Instead, they formed a huddle.

"This is a dilemma," Ned said. "They are both funny. But Roger often uses his humor as a type of passive-aggressive manipulation."

Boomer nodded. "Ah, but Doug can deal with Roger's deep-seated hostility and he won't attack *us*."

That settled it. "Duh . . . let's sit with Doug," Willy suggested.

The three boys took seats near Doug. Roger couldn't believe it. His gang had deserted him for Doug Funnie!

At lunchtime, Doug kept his new friends laughing as they ate.

"Boy, I'll bet this food keeps the school nurse busy," Doug teased as he stared at the pile of mystery meat on his plate. "They're selling stomach pumps in the lobby!"

Ned, Willy, and Boomer roared. Willy laughed so hard, orange juice came out his nose!

Doug kept joking all day long. As they passed the teachers' lounge on the way back to class, Doug said, "Boy! We do all the work, and they get paid!"

Ned, Willy, and Boomer laughed again— only not so hard this time.

After school, Doug and his gang stopped at the flagpole. "Some school colors," Doug said. "My TV looks like that when it's on the blink."

This time, Ned, Willy, and Boomer didn't laugh at all.

"I thought you guys said he was funny," Willy complained.

"What happened, Doug?" Ned asked.

"How come you're not funny anymore?" Boomer added.

Doug gulped. Funnieman was bombing!

Chapter 5

That evening, Doug sat alone in his room. He imagined he was Funnieman again. But this time, his fantasy wasn't funny. It was a nightmare. Funnieman's jokes were bad. Even in Doug's dreams, he couldn't make the audience laugh.

"I've got it," he told his dog, Porkchop. "If brains were pennies, you wouldn't have any sense."

Porkchop let out a huge laugh. But Doug wasn't fooled. "You're humoring me, aren't you?"

Porkchop stopped laughing and shrugged. Doug sighed. He couldn't even make his own dog laugh.

"It's no use, Porkchop," Doug moaned.

"I've lost it."

Doug stood by his window and looked out into the warm night. Down below his room, Doug could hear his father talking to their neighbor, Mr. Dink.

"Say, Bud," Doug's father said. "How's Tippy? We haven't seen much of her since she was elected mayor."

"Me neither," Mr. Dink replied. "I'm so miserable without her, it's almost like having her here!"

Doug's father and Mr. Dink laughed like it was a funny joke.

"Gee," Doug said to Porkchop. "If only I could tell a put-down joke like that. Mr. Dink makes it seem so easy."

That was it. The only way Doug was going to learn how to tell a good joke was to learn from a master. Doug obviously had a master living right next door.

Doug raced over to the Dinks' and rang the bell.

23

"Douglas, my boy," Mr. Dink greeted him as he opened the door. "Come in, come in. To what do I owe the pleasure of this visit?"

Doug and Porkchop followed Mr. Dink into the living room. "Well, I heard what you said about Mrs. Dink," Doug began.

Mr. Dink got very uncomfortable. Beads of sweat formed on his forehead. "That was just a little joke," he said nervously. "Nothing you would ever want to repeat to the missus."

"Oh no, Mr. Dink," Doug assured him. "It's just that I need to know how to tell a joke like that."

Mr. Dink gave a big sigh of relief. Then

he walked over to a wooden cabinet and pulled out a round reel of film. Doug had never seen anything like it before.

"Gee, what's that?" Doug asked.

"A Super-8 movie," Mr. Dink explained. "Kind of a prevideo video. We used to project them on a screen with one of these projectors." Mr. Dink pointed to a large metal machine with two circular reels on it.

"Gee thanks, Mr. Dink," Doug said with a disappointed tone, "but I don't think we have one of those projector thingies."

Mr. Dink glanced at the clock. Uh oh! His wife would be home any minute. And she did not like the movie Mr. Dink was talking about.

"Tell you what, Douglas," Mr. Dink said. "Take the projector and the screen. You can watch the movie at home."

Mr. Dink loaded the movie reels, the big metal projector, and a long white movie screen into Doug's arms. Doug managed to

mutter a thank-you as he walked out the door.

"Don't mention it, Douglas," Mr. Dink called after him. "Ever. Especially not to the missus!"

Chapter 6

That night, Doug sat on his bed and watched reel after reel of movies starring the old-time comedian Rick Nickles. He was the king of comedy in *his* day. He had a million jokes!

"My mother-in-law is so dumb she could get lost in a revolving door," Rick Nickles barked. Doug grinned. This was just the material he was looking for.

As Doug watched the rest of the movie, he saw himself telling Rick Nickles's jokes. "And speaking of fat," Doug told his imaginary audience, "she was so fat, she was named Miss North Dakota, South Dakota, and a little bit of Montana."

People would go wild for this stuff.

The next morning, Doug was ready to take on the world. It was Saturday, and Doug knew everyone would be at Swirly's. He could try out his new routine.

"Come on, Porkchop," Doug urged.

Porkchop started for the door. Doug looked behind him, clicked his tongue, and said, "Gee, Porkchop, if you gain any more weight, you'll have to turn your mirror sideways!"

Porkchop stopped. He looked nervously at his stomach.

Doug laughed and walked out the door. "Come on, Porkchop, lighten up. It was just a joke!"

By the time Doug and Porkchop arrived at Swirly's, most of the kids were already there. Willy, Ned, and Boomer slid over in their booth and made room for Doug. Roger sat in a nearby booth—by himself.

"There's Roger, sitting with all his friends," Doug teased in a voice loud enough for everyone to hear. Willy, Ned, and Boomer laughed.

Doug kept at it. "I don't know what's eating him, but it must have indigestion!"

Roger's face turned red with anger. His fingers drummed nervously on the tabletop.

Just then, Skeeter walked over to Doug's table. "Hey, Doug," he said, "I thought you were gonna meet me at my house."

Doug looked sheepishly at Skeeter. He'd been so excited about all his new jokes that he'd forgotten. "Sorry, Skeet," Doug apologized. "Take a load off."

Skeeter looked at the booth. All the seats were taken. "Where am I supposed to sit?" he asked.

"Oh. There's no room," Doug replied.

"Why don't you sit over there with Roger? Plenty of room at his table!"

Willy, Ned, and Boomer started to snicker. Skeeter looked curiously at Doug. "Huh?"

Doug looked at his new group of friends. Then he looked at Skeeter. "I-I said sit with Roger," Doug repeated nervously. "If you've had your shots, that is. Woof! Woof!"

The gang laughed really hard. So hard that Willy choked on his milkshake. Skeeter just walked away, confused.

Doug watched Skeeter leave. He could tell that his friend was upset. But Doug couldn't think about that right now. He was Funnieman, the King of Insults.

Now, wherever Doug went, Willy, Ned, and Boomer followed. So, when Doug went to watch Patti play baseball, they sat beside him on the bleachers.

As usual, Patti was playing really well. She had already led the team to a huge lead in the sixth inning. But that didn't seem to be enough for Chalky.

"Come on, people, stay awake out there!" he yelled at his teammates. "We blew the shutout. They're gaining on us."

"We're winning fifteen to one, Chalky," Patti reminded him as she picked up a bat and headed for the plate.

Thwack! Patti swung the bat and hit a long one. She ran to first and then slid into second for a double.

Doug cheered wildly. He was so busy watching Patti, he didn't notice that Roger had showed up—with three new friends in tow.

Willy, Ned, and Boomer watched as Roger pulled out a wad of cash and started buying souvenirs for his new friends.

Willy said, "Duh. It looks like Roger has a new gang."

"And he's buying them everything in sight!" Ned added.

Doug got nervous. Roger was buying friends. Roger had a lot of money. What if he wanted to buy back his old friends, too?

Doug had to do something . . . fast. But what?

Just then Doug spotted Skeeter sitting on

the bench. He cupped his hands and yelled down to him.

"Hey, Skeeter, buddy! Way to keep the bench warm. What position are you playing? Left out?"

Doug's plan worked like a charm. Willy, Ned, and Boomer stopped watching Roger, and started laughing with Doug. Doug was so relieved he didn't even notice the sad expression on Skeeter's face.

Chapter 7

Doug's reputation as the King of Insults really grew. Soon kids he didn't even know were waving to him in the hall. It was a feeling Doug had never experienced before. Doug couldn't stop his put-down jokes—even if he wanted to.

Late one afternoon, Ms. Kristal gave the class a new book to read.

"I am assigning this book because it was my favorite when I was your age," she explained.

"Only now it's not printed on stone tablets," Doug whispered to his gang of pals.

Ms. Kristal heard Doug, and she tried to laugh. "I used to spend hours reading in my room," she continued.

"Yeah, by candlelight," Doug interrupted.

The gang laughed even louder.

Ms. Kristal tried to ignore them. "I love books, because they take me to places I've never been before."

"Like planet Earth!" Doug joked. The class roared. Ms. Kristal looked like she was about to cry.

"I think we've had enough today," she said softly. "Class dismissed."

As the kids left the classroom, Boomer looked at Doug with awe.

"Wow, Doug," he exclaimed. "I think you made the teacher cry!"

"Yeah," Willy added. "I don't even think Roger's done that."

Doug looked back into the classroom. Sure enough, Ms. Kristal was resting her head in her hands. She looked like she was really crying. Now Doug was confused. Nobody ever cried when Rick Nickles told *his* jokes.

What was Doug doing wrong?

Chapter 8

After school, Willy, Ned, and Boomer came over to Doug's house. They didn't have any real plans, they were just hanging out—as a gang. Doug asked Skeeter if he wanted to come over, too, but Skeeter said he had something else to do. Doug thought Skeeter seemed mad at him.

Doug tried not to think about Skeeter as he sat down with his new friends for some of Mrs. Funnie's double-decker chocolate cake and a glass of milk.

"Here you are, boys," Mrs. Funnie said, as she served each of the boys a huge slice of cake. "A nice big slice for each of you. And I saved a little sliver for myself."

The guys snickered. They figured this was the perfect setup for one of Doug's put-down jokes. Doug gulped. Was he supposed to goof on his own mother?

Willy poked Doug in the side. That was exactly what the guys wanted him to do.

"Yeah, right, Mom," Doug said. "You eat like a bird—a really big bird."

Mrs. Funnie looked shocked. Doug's friends tried to hold back their laughter, but they couldn't. Willy laughed so hard, pieces of chocolate cake flew out of his mouth.

Doug tried hard not to look at the hurt expression on his mother's face.

After they'd finished their cake, Ned, Boomer, and Willy wanted to hear more of Doug's jokes. But there was no one else home in the Funnie house. So they told Doug they wanted to go in search of more people for Doug to goof on. They figured everyone was at the bowling alley.

Patti was the first person Doug saw as he went in. She was sitting at a lane with her two friends, Connie and Beebe. He led his gang to the lane right next to Patti's.

"Hey, Patti! Hey, Connie. Hey, Beebe," Doug said to the girls shyly. Doug always got a little shy when he was near Patti.

"Hey, Doug," Patti answered as she got up to take her turn.

Doug watched as Patti picked up her ball and headed for the line.

Boomer tripped and Doug immediately shot off with, "Hey, nice trip. See you in the fall." The gang laughed.

Patti turned around and looked at Boomer. "Could you keep it down?"

she asked. "You're ruining my concentration."

Boomer put his hands on his hips, puckered his lips, and said in a supersarcastic voice, "You're ruining my reputation."

That made Patti mad. And when she was mad, Patti could really bowl! *Crash!* The ball went soaring down the lane, knocking down all ten pins.

Patti punched her fist in the air. "I won! I won! Yes!" she cheered.

Ned watched as Patti smiled. "Come on, Doug," he urged. "Get her!"

Oh no! Get Patti? *Patti?* Doug looked anxiously at Willy, Ned, and Boomer. They were waiting with anticipation.

"It's a good thing she won," Doug said, finally. "I'm not saying she's a sore loser, but *she* gets mad when she loses her breath!"

The guys liked that one. They laughed harder than ever. "Atta boy, Doug," Boomer said. "Let her have it."

Doug nodded and went in for the kill.

"She's such a sorehead, it's a wonder her hair's not black and blue!"

Patti looked at Doug and gasped. Doug was her friend! How could he say something so mean? She grabbed her things and stormed out.

Doug jumped up. He was frantic. "Patti,

wait!" he cried out over the sound of crashing pins. "I didn't mean it! It was just a joke!"

But Patti didn't answer.

Willy, Ned, and Boomer were really laugh-

41

ing now. "Will you guys can it!" Doug exclaimed. The boys stopped laughing, instantly.

"Hey, what's your problem?" Boomer asked Doug.

Doug stared at the bowling-alley door. "Why don't you guys just leave me alone," he muttered sadly.

Willy, Ned, and Boomer stood up. "Gladly!" Boomer exclaimed.

"It's not as if *we* don't have feelings," Ned said.

"Duh, he's mean!" Willy agreed.

Chapter 9

The next day, Doug went to the baseball field by himself. Beebe Bluff was playing Cheeseburg Middle School. Usually, the Beebe Bluff team creamed Cheeseburg. But today that would be tough. Most of the Beebe Bluff team was on strike.

"What do you mean 'on strike'?" Doug heard Chalky ask Patti.

"You can go by yourself," Patti replied. "We've had enough. You took all the fun out of the game."

"But we won!" Chalky insisted. He watched as Patti shrugged and went back to the picket line. "Fine then!" Chalky declared. "I'll do it myself!"

Doug sat alone at the top of the bleachers. For the first time the whole season, Beebe Bluff Middle School was losing! Doug watched as Chalky wound up for his pitch. He threw the ball. The batter slammed the pitch way out to left field. Chalky ran to the outfield, grabbed the ball on the fifth bounce, and raced frantically to home plate, sliding in just after the runner.

"*Safe!*" the umpire called.

"It's pathetic," Doug said to himself. "Chalky's trying to play the game all by himself." Then Doug looked around at the empty seats around him. "And I know exactly how he feels."

Doug kept his eyes on the game, but he wasn't really watching. He was thinking of himself as a very, very old man. Same hair, same shorts, same T-shirt. Just very, very old.

In his mind Doug could see two frightened

kids. They'd lost their Whacky Wizzer in Old Man Doug's hedge. Now they were trying to figure out which of them would have to go get it.

"Let's go together," the girl suggested.

The girl and boy raced into the yard, grabbed their Whacky Wizzer, and ran for their lives. But before they could make it past the gate, mean Old Man Doug sprayed them with water.

"Are you kids in my yard or was I just watering the weeds?" Old Man Doug said.

The imaginary kids ran away in fear.

The thought of little kids hating him snapped Doug back to reality. He couldn't let that happen to him.

That night, Doug couldn't sleep. "What's happening to me?" he asked Porkchop.

"What kind of guy am I, anyway? I've insulted everyone I know. Even Patti! She'll never speak to me again!"

Porkchop looked up at Doug and pointed out the window to Mr. Dink's house.

Doug knew what he had to do. He began packing up the movie projector, the screen, and all of Mr. Dink's Rick Nickles movie reels.

"I gotta give this stuff back to Mr. Dink before it ruins my life!"

As he got back into bed, Doug sighed, "I'm gonna have a busy day tomorrow."

Chapter 10

The next morning, Doug was up with the sun. The smell of homemade waffles drifted up the stairs and into his room. Quickly, Doug pulled on his clothes and raced downstairs.

"Mom, I'm sorry I insulted you yesterday," he apologized. "I don't know what got into me."

Doug's mother hugged her son. She forgave him. Doug breathed a sigh of relief. That wasn't so bad. But Doug had many more apologies to make before the day was over.

Doug got to school early so he could talk to Ms. Kristal in private. "I was trying to be funny, but I guess I was being mean," Doug explained. Ms. Kristal smiled. She wasn't angry or upset anymore.

Skeeter was the next one on Doug's apology list. Right after school, Doug went to Skeeter's house. Skeeter didn't even want to *see* Doug, never mind let him in his room. But Doug insisted. And when Skeeter heard Doug wanted to apologize, he gave in.

"At first I was just trying to stop Roger from picking on everybody. But then I got carried away," Doug explained when the two boys were finally alone in Skeeter's room. "I thought if I was funny, it would make everybody like me."

"Gee, Doug," Skeeter replied. "You didn't have to do all that. Most everybody *did* like you."

Doug was shocked. "They did?" he asked Skeeter.

"Well, at least nobody hated you," Skeeter corrected himself. He stood up and put on his jacket. "Come on, Doug," Skeeter urged. "Let's go to Swirly's."

Doug was a little nervous. He wasn't quite ready to go to Swirly's yet. There would

be a lot of people there. Most of them probably thought he was a real jerk!

Skeeter handed
Doug a pair of funny
eyeglasses with a fake
nose and a big, bushy
mustache. That made
Doug laugh. He
jumped up and put
his arm around his
best friend.

"You bet, Skeet," he answered. "My treat!"

Doug was right. Swirly's was packed and
kids were sick of Doug. In fact, the first people Doug ran into were Willy, Ned, and
Boomer. They were hanging out in the parking lot. Before Doug could say anything to
them, a huge stretch limo pulled up. The
chauffeur opened the door, and Roger
stepped out.

"Hey, Valentine," Roger called over to

Skeeter, "if you're going to hang out with Funnie, you need to wear one of these." Roger reached into the pocket of his black leather jacket and pulled out a T-shirt. The shirt said I'M WITH STUPID.

"See," Roger said, pushing the shirt into Skeeter's face. "It says, 'I'm with stupid.'"

Everyone in the parking lot looked at Doug.

"This is going to be good!" Willy whispered to Boomer.

Doug could think of a million really good comebacks for that T-shirt. Like, "I'm not going to engage in a battle of the wits with you. I never attack an unarmed man."

But Doug didn't say that because he was sick and tired of insulting people. He turned to Roger, smiled, and said:

"Oh yeah?"

Chapter 11

Ned, Boomer, and Willy stared at Doug with disbelief. Had he just said what they thought he'd said?

"Boy, that was *weak*!" Boomer exclaimed.

"Whoever said that guy was funny?" Ned asked.

Roger smiled triumphantly. He opened the door to his limo. "Hey, you guys want to come to my house?" he asked Ned, Willy, and Boomer.

Willy looked him in the eye. "I thought you had a new gang."

Roger shook his head. "Those losers were just after my money. Hop in the limo and I'll give you some free stuff."

"Wow!"

"Cool!"

"All right!" The gang jumped in and they drove away with Roger. Doug had thought he would be upset if the guys went back to being Roger's friends, but he wasn't. He realized that Ned, Boomer, and Willy weren't his friends at all. They just liked hearing him rank on people.

Doug took a deep breath, turned, and walked toward Swirly's. It was time for him to make the toughest apology of all.

Doug searched the restaurant. He finally spotted the person he was looking for—Patti. She was sitting by herself in a booth. Slowly, Doug approached her.

"Hey Patti, can I sit down?" he asked.

Patti looked unsure. But she said, "I guess so."

Doug sat down. "I'm really sorry I insulted you at the bowling alley," he said nervously.

"That's okay, Doug," Patti replied gently.

"No. It's not," Doug admitted. "I was acting like a big jerk, insulting everybody. I guess a joke isn't funny unless everybody gets to laugh."

Just then Skeeter walked over with a tray of food. "You guys friends again?" he asked Doug and Patti.

Doug held a make-believe cigar up to his mouth and pretended to be an old-time comedian. "Come on, Patti," he urged in a silly voice, "don't be a sorehead."

Patti touched her hair and stifled a

giggle. "Oh no!" she teased. "Is my hair turning black and blue?"

Doug smiled. He was forgiven. He stuck out his hand. "Friends?" he asked.

Patti shook his hand. "Friends," she

answered. "Well, I better go. Tomorrow's the championship game." .

"You mean the strike is over?" Doug asked as he got up to let Patti out of the booth.

Patti nodded. "Yeah. Chalky promised to lighten up and have some fun. I guess he learned his lesson the hard way."

Doug laughed. He knew just how that felt.

Chapter 12

The next day, Doug sat in the stands watching the championship game. Chalky was sitting this game out, too. He'd gotten pretty banged up playing a whole game by himself.

Patti stepped up to bat. The pitch flew by. It was a little low and inside, but she swung. *Crack.* The ball flew toward center field. Base hit.

"Way to go, Patti!" Chalky cheered from the dugout. "Nice hit."

New Hamster was one tough team. Their pitcher struck out the next three batters. As the New Hamster team went to bat, the score was tied eleven to eleven in the ninth inning. It was now or never.

"Hey, Skeeter," Chalky called. "I need you."

Skeeter hopped up from his spot on the bench. "More water?" he asked. "Bandages?"

Chalky shook his head. "I need you to go out there and strike this guy out."

Skeeter jumped up excitedly. "Really? No kidding, Chalky?" he asked.

Chalky nodded. Skeeter jogged out to the mound. He took the ball from Patti and warmed up with the catcher.

Finally, the batter stepped into the box and Skeeter pitched the ball. It flew over the 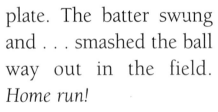 plate. The batter swung and . . . smashed the ball way out in the field. *Home run!*

"Wow!" Skeeter exclaimed. "Anyone ever see a ball hit that far?"

That was it. The game was over. The New Hamster team were the champions. But Chalky wasn't letting that get him down.

"You guys are the best team any captain ever had," Chalky told them, "even if we did lose the championship and we're only number two!"

The team lifted Chalky high on their shoulders.

"We're number two! We're number two!" they chanted.

Doug stood on the sidelines, watching the celebration. Patti turned and called to him.

"Come on, Doug. We're all going to Swirly's," she shouted over the cheers.

"Yeah, come on, Doug," Chalky agreed.

"Well, everything's back to normal," Doug said to himself. Just then, Willy, Ned, and Boomer followed Roger out of the stadium.

"Outta my way, loser," Willy said, bumping into Doug.

"Yeah, what a loser," Roger agreed. He darted toward his limo. Willy, Ned, and Boomer ran close behind. *Umph!* The three boys bashed into Roger and collapsed in a heap next to the limo.

"Hey, watch it, you losers!" Roger shouted as he tried to dig his way out of the pile of arms and legs.

"Yep, everything's back to normal," Doug chuckled and he ran off to join his friends.